About the Author

Marcus C. Stanley, thirty-six-year-old educator from Atlanta, GA.

What About Charlie?

Marcus C. Stanley

What About Charlie?

Olympia Publishers
London

www.olympiapublishers.com
OLYMPIA PAPERBACK EDITION

Copyright © Marcus C. Stanley 2022

A CIP catalogue record for this title is
available from the British Library.

ISBN: 978-1-80074-361-8

First Published in 2022

Olympia Publishers
Tallis House
2 Tallis Street
London
EC4Y 0AB
Printed in Great Britain

Dedication

I would like to dedicate this book to myself, for finally putting me first.

Acknowledgements

I would like to thank Her for giving me the wisdom and time to write this book.

Chapter 1

"What about Charlie?" I ask.

"It's your dog, Lauren, you keep him."

Before I could say that I didn't even ask for the dog, Simon slams the door, startling Charlie. I am not going to cry. This is what needs to happen, I tell myself, as I listen to the elevator ding, letting me know that Simon is leaving me twice. I wish that he would get stuck in there for as long as he kept me in this relationship.

That's three long, worthless years of waiting for him to want to settle down. Geesh, he wouldn't even move in together. I'm twenty-five — how much longer am I going to have to wait? I mean, thirty is creeping up on me. Most of my friends are getting married.

My thoughts are interrupted when Charlie walks between my legs. He startles me as the tears began to fall. I can get over Simon I tell myself; I've wasted so much time on us. No one wants to be the girl that has no one. People will think I'm damaged goods.

I flop down on my sofa. My soft, blue-gray sofa. The sofa I picked out with Wade, my best friend, because Simon was too busy with work to come with me.

Before I could get comfortable, Charlie, my two-year-old Golden Retriever, comes over. He is so calm and loving, unlike other labs I've seen at Piedmont Park or on the Atlanta Beltline. He has one green eye and one blue eye. Simon got him for us this past Christmas. I think he only got me the dog because I complained about him leaving me alone too much. I only agreed to keep Charlie if Simon paid for him to be professionally trained — something he reluctantly agreed to.

Since Christmas, it's been Charlie and me for the most part. Wade occasionally joins us on walks and trips to Ponce City Market. Charlie and I watch a morning news show at 6:30 a.m. She begins with news about this coronavirus from China. This seems so unreal. As she goes over more stats and data, my phone rings right on cue at 6:45 a.m.

Wade says, "Good morning, sleepyhead. I hope you took care of that morning breath."

"Fuck you," I reply.

He laughs out loud. "I hope you don't kiss your mother with that mouth." I go silent.

He clearly senses I'm annoyed because I am not ready for his antics this morning. "I'm sorry, L.A."

L.A. is his nickname for me. He is the only person I ever told my full name: Lauren Anastasia Peterson. To everyone else, I am just Lauren Peterson. I hate my middle name. My mother let my older sister, Tabitha, name me and that Anastasia was her favorite character. Who even knows that story?

He asks, "what's wrong?" I didn't even get to say anything before he added, "Let me guess, Simon left this morning with a performance worth a SAG nomination."

"Ding, ding, ding," I reply.

"L.A., why do you —"

I didn't let him start on his weekly tangent about how bad Simon has treated me and how I deserve someone who appreciates me. "We're done."

He pauses. "Really?" he says sarcastically.

"Yes, we're done."

"Like Cardi B and Offset done or like—"

I don't need his comedic roast about my love life. I shout, "No, done like you and me — you remember, right? How you dumped me our senior year of college? Done!"

"L.A., I'm sorry—"

I end the call and toss my phone across the room. It lands on the giant bean bag chair I bought hoping that Simon and I could cuddle and Netflix and chill on.

"Fuck my life!" I yell.

Charlie to raises his head. I'm glad he's here, so warm and cozy on my lap. At this point, Charlie is the man for me.

I lay back, trying to sort through all the thoughts going through my head. But I remember that I have to get dressed for work. I tap Charlie to move and jump up to return to the bathroom, with him not far behind.

The water is running and the sink is full of hair from King Hairy the Third. I smile. He hated when I called him that. I wash my face and brush my teeth.

I walk out just in time to hear the weather report and it was going to be a cool and sunny day for February in Atlanta.

I grab a pair of my footed, black designer leggings, a black pencil skirt and a white blouse before I head to my second-grade class.

Chapter 2

I sit in the car as it warms. I brush my blonde hair into a ponytail, apply a thin layer of mascara onto my eyelashes and apply lipstick then lip gloss. Somehow, car mirrors are the best for applying makeup.

As I head onto I-285, I think about Wade. Maybe I was too harsh on him this morning. What I said was true but it wasn't the whole truth. Wade and I were the perfect couple. He was attractive, funny, loving, attentive. The sex was amazing but, like most men, he wasn't ready to settle down and get married. Wade was a great communicator. He always told me how he was feeling. I didn't have to wonder what he was thinking because he told me.

It was March of our senior year at Auburn University. I had an off-campus apartment on Colombia Drive. Wade and I spent every night together, either at his place or mine. It seemed as if my life was on the perfect track. I was on cruise control, not struggling like some of the other students scrambling for internships and cramming for exams. I had a solid 3.4 GPA and was looking forward to my interviews in the upcoming weeks for a teaching position with Dekalb County Public Schools.

I was in desperate need of sex after just getting back from my spring break trip that I took with some girls from campus.

Whilst I was unpacking, I heard the knock on the door. knew it was Wade. I opened the door and jumped into his arms.

"Hey, L.A.," he said, "how was your trip?"

I was so ready to undress him that I didn't even hear him talking. I was just getting down on my knees to give him the best blowjob of his life when he stopped me.

"We need to talk."

Now, this wasn't big, since Wade was an excellent communicator. But I got that pit in the stomach feeling so I knew this was about to be bad, but how bad?

I stood up feeling so rejected. He looked me in the eyes, like he always does, but, this time, there were tears. Which immediately made me have tears in my eyes.

He said, "Lauren, I love you... but I want to make sure we are right for each other. You're the only woman I've ever loved and, before I can commit to you, I want to date other women. I want to know if the love I have for you is real. I've never had any other serious relationship outside of you. I don't ever want to have any regrets. Lauren. I want to know, if I'm a different person when I'm around someone else. Most of all, I want to know what it's like not to have you in my life, to see if it's the same."

I was speechless. My mouth was open, but nothing came out.

"Lauren... Lauren... Lau—"

"I heard you," I say quietly. But the room was so quiet that you would have heard a fly land on the window sill.

He began talking again but all I remember doing was walking over to my suitcase and handing him the custom t-shirt and shot glass that had our names with hearts on it from one of those strip shops on the Panama City beach. I hugged him and he left.

That day was the worst day of my life. I'd had so many things planned for the two of us. How could he do this?

My thoughts are interrupted when Bert Weiss from the Bert Show began discussing with a caller on how to get closure from an ex. I quickly change the station. Usually, I'm for the drama but, after the morning I've had, I'm not in the mood for hearing anyone else's bad news.

At 7:37 a.m., I park into the faculty parking lot at Oakhurst Elementary School. I grab my purse and then I remember that I didn't leave any water or food for Charlie. I'm such a horrible person, I tell myself. Thinking how hungry Charlie is going to be having to wait all day to eat, I debate going back home but, with the traffic in Atlanta, it would easily add two hours to my trip.

This is all Simon's fault. If he would have not been so moody when I asked whether he was going with me to my friend Megan's wedding, then none of this would have happened. Simon is a guy who hates weddings because he thinks every woman wants to trap him into getting married. That was never my intention. I wanted to get married but not at the expense of tricking someone into it. I just wanted a date — not go alone and look like an absolute loser.

I check my makeup and gather all my belongings. I try my best to put on my big girl smile, to not look like my heart was just shattered into a million pieces.

Chapter 3

The day went fast, thank God. The children, for a Thursday, were pretty calm and the principal didn't even hold the staff meeting for the entire hour.

God does love me, considering how my morning went.

I check my phone; there is no signal inside the walls of this old school — walls which I'm pretty sure are painted with lead paint. I see that I have a few text messages and two missed calls.

I secretly want it to be Simon apologizing for being such a jerk but I know that would never happen.

Four messages are from Wade apologizing and saying that he's bringing me Zoe's Kitchen and Pinot Noir for dinner. He knows I couldn't say no to chicken kabobs and red wine.

Another text is reminding me to register to vote. Who gave these guys my number? There's a text from my mom just checking in and, lastly, a reminder about Charlie's graduation from Obedience School.

Charlie! This reminds me to hurry home to feed and walk him.

"Charlie," I call as I approach the front door. I can see his shadow from underneath the door. I unlock the door and he is excited to see me. I quickly change from high heel shoes to multi- colored tennis shoes that I bought strictly for walking Charlie. Now that I'm newly single, I might meet a guy that is into sneakers.

Charlie and I head out the door because keeping the carpet clean comes before food and water. We walk into the elevator and he looks at me like he knows I'm sad on the inside. I rub his head as if I'm telling him that I am okay and he licks my hand. It was warm and tacky. It had felt weird at first but my hand, over the past months, has gotten used to it.

We head out. He takes care of business then we head back up.

I turn on the tv to CNN before I head to the kitchen to fix Charlie's food that is long overdue. I give him a little extra since he hasn't eaten all day. I pour myself a glass of wine to begin my afternoon wind down and cut a few slices of cheese I had in the refrigerator. This should hold me over until Wade gets here with dinner.

More news about the coronavirus. I watch in awe as I see countries begin shutting down their entire cities, leaving the streets empty.

"This reminds me of a movie," I say.

Charlie strolls into the room after finishing his dinner.

"That was fast," I joke as he returns to his position on the couch and lays his head on my lap. I rub him and say: "Sorry for not feeding you. It's stupid Simon's fault but I will never let it happen again."

Charlie looks at me with the one blue eye and one green eye. It's like he can read my mind.

"Yeah, you're right, screw that loser."

The doorbell rings an hour later while Charlie and I are bingeing the news, absorbing all the facts about this terror called corona.

Charlie jumps up, barks and rushes towards the door. Simon hated when he did that. I actually felt more protected by Charlie than I ever did with Simon. I mean, honestly, if a guy tried to mug me whilst I was with Simon, he would probably run faster than me with his skinny jeans, and V-neck sweater. I would've had to fight for myself.

I walk over to the peep hole and see Wade there holding flowers.

"Where's Zoe?"

He slowly holds up the bag and I open the door. I stand there, almost wanting him to get on his knees like the subs did in Fifty Shades of Grey books, but that would be too much. The thought of Wade taking me from behind would definitely help me relieve some stress. I'm already two glasses of wine in — this kitty is already in pre-heat.

Wade walks in — his sexy self, standing at about six feet, in a nice custom, blue suit and a white shirt with a blue tie. The suit accentuated his arms that look good from all the years of playing baseball.

"You must have had a meeting today," I say as I take some of the bags from his hand, only what looks like my food and wine.

He says yes and then takes off his shoes and has on a nice pair of blue and brown socks. Simon never wore matching socks.

His voice brings me back to earth. "Hey Charlie, how are you today?"

Charlie stares for a second, almost looking annoyed that his lap time was interrupted, then turns and heads to his pillow that was placed in the corner of the living room. I love how he talks to Charlie like a person, instead of the dumb baby talk people do when taking to dogs.

"Enough about me; let's talk about you," says Wade, "I want to really apologize for being so inconsiderate this morning. I didn't take your feelings seriously. I know I joke a lot but this morning I clearly went too far. Do you want to talk about it?"

Not really but because you brought food I'll share. I briefly go over the details of the argument. That started by simply asking if Simon would be attending Megan's wedding with me. I will never know how the question led to him of accusing me of trying to trap him into a marriage.

I will never know how that escalated into a big fight."

Wade asks, "What makes this different from the other times he's stormed out?"

"I don't know. I feel like this is the end. I can't force anyone to be with me — besides, he hasn't called or texted me all day and I am completely okay with that."

That reminds me of Mom's text that I did not reply to. I grab my phone and text: 'I'm fine dinner, with Wade at my house. Call you tomorrow.'

Mom and I speak every day. We have a really great relationship and I want to keep it that way.

"So, that's it?" he asked.

"Yes, Now, can we please eat? My pita bread is getting cold."

He laughs and grabs the bags, heading to the kitchen to put the food on plates because he knows how much I hate eating out of the containers from restaurants. They just sit there collecting dust until food is put into them. Gross.

As soon as Wade enters the kitchen, Charlie comes to join me on the couch. "Hey," I say, "Did you miss me?" His tail wags as he buries his head into my neck, wanting all of my attention.

I yell to Wade, "You need any help?"

"No!" This is mainly because he helped me move in here three years ago and knows the place like the back of his hand. He even got me a great deal on the place as he is an architect and knew the owners of the building, talking them into giving me 20k off my condo here in Sandy Springs.

I think that was his way of apologizing for the way he dumped me our senior year. I was grateful but would have loved it more if we moved in together.

"Oom-pah," he yells as he walks in with the food and balancing the wine glasses on the plate. Ugh, he loves showing off, and he looks good doing it.

Down girl I tell myself to keep me from jumping up and kissing Wade. Charlie jumps down off the sofa and goes to his pillow.

We turn on the TV. I ask him about the coronavirus thing and we discuss it. We talk about our day and about a book he was reading. It felt great to have communication and in-depth conversation which Wade always brought.

I communicate with Charlie more than I ever did with Simon. Ugh, what a waste. But I still wish he would text or call.

Wade stands, stretches and says, "Okay, L. A, I'm out. You're trying to keep me here all night."

"What do you mean?" I ask cluelessly.

"It's warm inside; we've both had three glasses of

wine. You're a sexy woman that is getting over a break up. This is a set up; I just need to exit before it gets messy in here."

I'm shocked that he said that. It made my kitty go from pre heat to damn near broil. He flashes a smile as I sit there with my mouth agape. He actually still likes me.

I get up to walk him to the door and hopefully he sees how hard my nipples are through my white t-shirt. As he reached down to get his shoes, I turn to show off my ass that peaks out my old cheer shorts that I could still fit in.

He laughs and says, "You're playing a dangerous game, L. A."

I turn on my southern bell accent. "Oh, whatever do you mean, good sir?"

He leans in. I close my eyes, and he kisses me on the forehead. "Good night, Lauren."

I'm so disappointed but I know Wade. He is a very controlled man — very precise in his words and actions.

He closes the door behind him. I lay with my face against the door, waiting for the elevator to ding. It does quickly for him. I wish it would have waited as long as it did for Simon.

It's 9 p.m. I've had five glasses of wine since 4 p.m. Nothing good is on TV, and I sure can't Netflix and chill. So, what is a girl to do?

That's right, masturbate. That kiss from Wade set off all my alarms and brought back so many memories.

I walk to my bed room with determination and I faintly hear footsteps behind me. Charlie.

"Sorry, Charlie, I need alone time."

I close the door in his face, feeling so guilty but desperately needing this release. Just give me five minutes, maybe ten. I may have to get off twice. Damn you, Wade.

I turn the light off and the tv on for background noise. I see the shadow of Charlie lying next to the door. I go to my square ottoman, which doubles as storage, to select from my collection of dildos and vibrators. I grab one of my many vibrators. A woman has to have options.

I lay on the bed and, with one click of a button, the wide head of the wand comes to life. It makes me sing a song that the heavens would approve of.

I think about the times Wade had come over during our senior year of college. Now, Wade did break up with me to essentially become a man-whore, but he made sure that I was on his roster. Instead of being the gentleman that took care of me and asked questions about my day, Wade was an animal. He was different. He wouldn't call or ask about my day but, instead, he would show up at my apartment unannounced and would fuck me senseless. He would bend me over and pound my small frame to pieces. I craved it and would anxiously wait to hear a knock on my door, hoping it would be him and his magic stick.

So, me wearing no bra and boy shorts tonight was nothing. I'd let Wade have me any way he wanted when we were together. I wanted him to know that I was his no matter what. If it took twenty years, this kitty would always purr for him.

I moan loudly as the vibrator sings its own tune, causing Charlie to stand on all fours that I see in between flashes of me opening my eyes in the darkness.

"Harder, Wade," I moan as if he was here.

With another click of a button, I think I have found

the meaning of life. It feels like I'm on fire but a good fire — the fire that tells you to keep going, knowing that it will burn. But it feels so good, like laying on the beach knowing you will get sun a burn.

This setting on the vibrator is buzzing a crazy rhythm that makes it hard to catch my breath. I grab the pillow and cover my face as I cum harder than I ever have before. I feel something wet falling on my thigh. I open my eyes to try to make out this wetness.

With legs shaking, I find enough strength to turn the light on and I see that I have squirted for the first time. I clean up my mess, clearly this is what Wade was talking about.

I grab my warm pajama pants, boots and blue jacket and prepare to walk Charlie. I should have planned better and walked Charlie first but, when you have the urge to cum, you have to cum. It's like the sexual desire takes control in the moment but, after you kill that urge, you come back to reality.

I sleepily walk to the elevator and head to the dog park area in my building. Charlie hates the cold as much as I do so this was a quick trip back upstairs and into the warm house.

We get back upstairs. I change the sheets and lay in bed thinking about the conversation I am going to have with my mother about Simon and me. Charlie jumps on the bed. I wrap my arms around him and fall asleep.

Chapter 4

My 6 AM alarm goes off.

I roll over to a warm body, thinking that my dream of Wade had come true, but nope, it's just Charlie. Which isn't bad but he just isn't Wade or Simon.

I grab my phone hoping to get a drunk text from Wade but it's just my mom replying 'okay' and Wade telling me that he made it home and thanking me for dinner. I hold down the loved button on my phone for both Wade and my mom's message.

I slip on my walking attire and turn on my coffee maker as Charlie and I head out. I got up a bit earlier this morning to clean up the mess I left last night and put the sheets in the dryer. Also, to make sure I did not forget to leave Charlie his food and water dish full.

I spoke to Wade briefly on the phone this morning, thanking him for dinner and the wonderful evening. He doesn't know that he put me to bed and I failed to mention the mess I made. LOL.

Feeling myself, I pull on my favorite blue sweater dress that makes my butt a little bigger and a pair of brown riding boots.

In the car I debate whether to call my mom in the car before work or after. I'll go with the latter.

I pull up to work with my coffee still hot. I think of Charlie, wondering which spot on the couch he is on.

I get out the car ready to tackle the day, even though I still haven't heard from Simon. I push that thought to the back of my mind and get ready to see the children that make me forget about my dating worries.

Today goes by even faster than expected. I love Thursday's or "Friday Eve" as I call it because my students and I both know that Fridays are chill days. I make sure to find a movie every Friday for the students to watch with the captions on and write down words that they don't know and I make look them up. That takes up most part of the morning and you add music class and lunch and Wala its 2:30 p.m.

Tomorrow is going to be a breeze, I tell myself.

I get home, take care of Charlie and prepare to tell my mother that Simon and I are on the outs for good. Mom, what am I supposed to do just sit and just be in a dead relationship like you and dad? I think to myself.

Don't get me wrong, my parents are together but their marriage is dead. Not a spark of romance or spontaneity. They are just two people existing, pretending to love each other. I want more than just a body in the house with me. After being married for thirty years. you would think that they would be head over heels but they are more like halfway in the grave.

"No," she says, "but you should learn to be more patient. Maybe Simon is not ready—"

"I get that, Mom." I interrupt her — something I hardly ever do because of her sound advice. But, when it comes to the dating department the survey says no thanks, Mom. "Simon is not marriage material, anyway. I am not even sure why he is so pressed about being married. I never gave him any ultimatums or even talked about marriage all the time. We spoke about it once a while back I told him my honest feelings. That I wanted to be married and have kids before I was twenty-seven. Each year we were together he began to get anxious and annoyed at the slightest mention of marriage. He wouldn't even watch Married at First Sight with me. Who is that afraid of marriage?" I tell my mom.

She lets out a sigh and is silent.

I pat Charlie's head which is buried in my lap. I'm starting to wonder if he has separation anxiety because he is so attached to me. Maybe he feels the loneliness inside me and is trying to make up for the lack of affection I'm getting from all the male counterparts in my life.

My mom wakes me from my thoughts and asks, "Well, did he take Charlie?"

"No," I say, thinking why does that matter.

My mom hears the dryness in my voice and says, "Well, honey, I know Charlie may not be a groom at the alter standing in a tux but he does offer love, companionship, stability, and comfort. It's only you and him for the mean time. You won't be stuck with Charlie forever and you always said you would much rather be with Wade. Don't forget about him. The way I see it, you have more options than you think you have."

I look at Charlie with his blue/green eye combination and say, "You're right, Mom."

I give Charlie a kiss on the nose and change the subject to the coronavirus news; we share our facts and what we've heard about cities' lockdowns. She made me promise to get groceries and to wash my hands and all the other stuff your parents tell you to do to stay safe and we end the call.

"What's for dinner?" I ask Charlie. He looks at me and shakes his head almost saying 'IDK'.

"Me either," I reply.

I open the Uber Eats app and decide on Chinese. I order enough lo Mein and shrimp and broccoli for lunch the next day and we watch an episode of Dynasty until the food arrives.

The doorbell rings and Charlie, with his protective self, lets out a bark that scares me. I rush to the door and open it to see a cute black guy holding my food. I had changed into my t-shirt and boy shorts so he is in for a little peep show for this one-minute interaction.

I grab the food and say, "Thank you."

He stands there in a bit of a daze after seeing my nipples through the shirt. He opens his mouth to say "Thank you, too," and I close the door.

Yup, I still got it. I do a little twerk that I could see in the long mirror I have in my bedroom. How the hell am I not married with at least one kid?

As I dance, Charlie jumps up and wants to dance, too. I put the food down and grab both his front paws and we dance in the living room to me making some music with my mouth. I knew that, if Simon were here, he would just look at me and ask what I was doing. He wasn't any fun. All he cared about was his dumb car. I hate that I even gave him my number when meeting him at the tire shop. I thought he looked cute so I didn't even notice how much he talked about his damn Ford Mustang with twin exhaust. How could I ever forget that day?

It was Summer of 2017. I was at the Goodyear Tire shop near my house, getting a nail from my car's tire. With all the construction that was going on in Atlanta, it's no telling where I picked that nail up from.

I was still on Wade's rotation but wanted more than just sex. I wanted companionship, loyalty, communication. I wanted a relationship. I was dating but nothing serious. Hoping that Wade would soon jump out of his HO, HO, HO, phase of life.

When I met Simon, he was really a rebound guy that turned long term. Simon dressed nicely and, apparently, I looked good in my cut off jean shorts and tank top. The wonderful tan, I had just gotten while on vacation in Cancun, made him come over while sitting in the quiet lobby.

He asked, "What are you in for," like we were in jail which was corny but cute.

I replied, "Nail in tire, looking at about five to ten minutes that is."

That made him laugh and I saw his pearly white teeth which was a turn on and he said he had a 2016 Mustang and that he did illegal street racing, I found that sexy and dangerous but he also had a real job as a Logistic Analyst at a trucking company.

We exchanged numbers and Instagram tags and went out to dinner the next day and the rest is a blur. We had some good times for the first 6 months like most relationships but, after the honeymoon phase is over and people showed their true colors, our relationship became full of arguments, missed celebrations and unfulfilled promises.

I didn't even get a WCW shout out on IG.

I was hoping that Wade seeing me with someone else on a full-time basis would make him jealous and want me back in no time. That's really the reason I stayed with him so long.

When I called and told Wade that I had met someone and that we were sexually active, he took me off the roster which I thought was unfair. Like how could you have your cake and eat it too but I can't?

Wade said it wasn't like that, that it was out of respect for the person that I was with. Which I understood because Wade scratched an itch that Simon could never reach. Wade then became like my best friend; we did everything together except having sex and, of course, that left me confused and Simon jealous.

Charlie and I finish shaking our booties and I put the food on the table and grab two plates. Then I remember that all this food is for me and that I am alone.

I begin to cry in the kitchen.

Like WTF, how did I go from flirting with the delivery guy to dancing to crying in the kitchen?

I've got to get it together. I wipe my tears with my wrist like a little kid and tell myself to calm down and breath.

Charlie walks over and squeezes between my legs and his soft fur causes me to relax. I thought about what my mom said about how Charlie was there to help and I should embrace that. So, I did just that. I rubbed him and told him that I loved him.

I fixed my plate and stopped crying.

Chapter 5

It's Saturday morning, my favorite day of the week. Charlie and I sleep in until 8 a.m. on the weekends which is much better than getting up at 6 a.m. every morning.

I walk into the living room in just my t-shirt. Who has time for panties?

I notice all the decorations I brought home from work yesterday. I didn't realize today was the 29th of February.

I pack them into their containers until next year and began to bring out the St Patrick Day decor to keep my classroom bright and vibrant for my kids and maybe bring some luck into my love life.

"I wish I had kids of my own," I say.

Just as that thought crosses my mind, Charlie reminds me it's time for his walk.

I grab my phone to text Tabitha. I told my mom last night that I would call her more. I text her: Hey, Tab's. Looking at the green bubble lets me know she still hasn't gotten an iPhone which makes it even more difficult to communicate. Maybe she's asleep?

I tell Charlie, "Today we are going shopping for his graduation outfit." I found a shop on Ponce that would make him a custom cap and gown. I was so excited and I actually sent out invitations, after taking my mom's advice, to a few family and friends to come and celebrate him.

I make my coffee and have avocado toast with scrambled egg and Charlie and I go for our morning walk. We head out onto Abernathy to walk towards the Sandy Spring performance art center but I notice there are less cars out than normal on a Saturday morning. I did hear on the news this morning that people are social distancing and not going out and that stores and businesses were closing because of the coronavirus. I noticed but wasn't going to let fear stop this new point in my life where I focus on myself. We walk our usual route and head back home.

I see that Tabitha has texted me back asking how I was doing and if I wanted to get dinner.

I decline and offer to have lunch after I picked up Charlies outfit. Tabitha wants to eat at Woody's Cheesesteaks while I opt for Arden's Garden which is within walking distance.

After grabbing our food, we sit outside because I have Charlie and talk.

She says, "I never liked Simon anyway," with her mouth full. You would have never thought that we were sisters. I mean, we are complete opposites. I'm somewhat together and she's falling apart. I mean she's gained so much weight since her divorce from Pete.

Pete loved Tabitha but wanted more from their marriage. With Tabitha being the oldest, she thinks my mom and dad's relationship was perfect so in her own marriage she applied the same energy, which was none. They didn't go on dates, vacations or anything romantic. Which is what she sees my parents doing, just existing with each other. Pete wanted the life of candlelit dinners and weekends in cabins but my sister only cared about her job and being at home. Pete tried counseling with her but, in the end, Tabitha was too stuck on stupid to really make her marriage work.

But, since the divorce, she has been getting out and supposedly working out, trying to find herself. Which I can't tell from the way she is eating this cheesesteak.

"I mean, he was a douche, Lauren. For God's sake, he raced cars. I'm glad you guys are over. He has hurt you too many times," Tabitha says.

I agree with her because every word is true. In a sad way, I realize at that moment I was going down the same path as my mom and dad in a useless relationship. The only thing was I wasn't married. The scary part of this is that if Simon would have asked me to marry him, I probably would have said yes and continued the cycle of bad relationships within my family. I sit quietly reflecting on my thoughts.

Tabitha asks, "Are you okay?"

I say, "Yes."

"You will be okay, don't worry." She reminds me of Wade and that makes me smile.

Tabitha quickly ruins the moment of bonding when she tosses a piece of meat to Charlie. I grab a napkin and pick it off the floor before he can eat it.

"Could you please not feed that to him?" I feed him an apple slice from my plate instead. I let it be known that I don't care what she thinks because Charlie is all mine and it feels good to think that. "So are you coming to his graduation?" I ask excitedly.

She says, "Yes," excitedly. "What gift should I bring?"

I show her the cart I have online for Charlie and she agrees to get him this new cooling pillow for pets. I tell her not to be late and send her the address.

Tabitha is a great sister. She's just... What's the word? Boring. She never wants to go to parties or hang out. She was always the responsible older sibling, who made great grades and now has an awesome career with tons of money as an engineer but no personality. She really took after my father.

My parents had Tabitha before they got married. Everyone thinks that's the reason they got married because there was clearly no real love between my parents.

We walk a bit on the beltline, mostly for her to walk off the whole cheesesteak she had. This was just for relaxation for Charlie and me since we had walked earlier this morning.

We talk about her recent therapy sessions that, I must admit, seem to be helping my sister. She seems a bit more confident and outgoing, maybe that was the reason why she didn't put up a fight when I asked her about attending the graduation. If it was this time last year, you would have thought I asked her to sit in the electric chair.

We share a few laughs and head back to our cars. I have to admit that this was the first time in a while that I actually had a great time with my sister.

Charlie hops in the front seat, I give him a hug and tell him how great he is and we head home for a nap.

Chapter 6

We're sad to inform you that, with the coronavirus spreading, we are postponing the graduation for the students at Roof Academy. We will reach out to you with another date and time in the near future. Signed Amy.

WTF. I just stare at the email on my work computer. It's after 3 p.m. but my principal called an emergency meeting about corona which everyone is taking about.

"What next," I say to myself. I text Wade to see if we we're still on for dinner plans.

As I walk towards the auditorium, I sit next to Ms Mitchell, another 2nd grade teacher that I work with.

"What do you think this is about?" she asks as if I have the slightest clue.

I reply. "I just hope it's nothing crazy."

"Ditto."

The auditorium is so loud to the point where the principal had to actually raise her voice to get everyone quiet.

"Now that I have your attention," she says under the horrible lighting in the auditorium. "Tomorrow you must take whatever belongings you need to complete your instruction for the next two weeks. Because of the spread of the coronavirus, all schools are being closed indefinitely for the next two weeks."

The once quiet auditorium now erupted with questions and comments.

"Quiet!" she yells as if she is a judge that misplaced her gavel and could no longer get control of her court.

Coach Bryan blows his whistle to get the crowd to a noise level that we could hear Principal Stewart speak.

"I know this is new to all of you but I trust that everyone will be fine. I will be sending out more information as it is told to me. But go home, get rest and tomorrow come in grab your things and prepare to work from home."

What does work from home look like, I'm a teacher? A million thoughts rush through my head.

I look down at my phone and see a text from Wade saying that he was going to have to rain check, because he had to get to the grocery store because everything seemed to be closing because of corona. I send him a text saying yes, go shopping and that I'm going home to grab Charlie and do the same. He sent a Heart emoji and said great idea and to call him when I got home.

A heart emoji? I haven't gotten that in a while. Could it be... Wade flirting?

I stop my thoughts and focus on the task at hand which was to get home, get Charlie and head to the grocery store. I make it home, run up, grab Charlie. I didn't change into my walking attire. He takes care of business and we load in the car.

My mom calls me as we're driving. "Hey, Lauren," she says with a bit of worry in her voice.

I quickly reply, "Mom, I'm okay."

She lets out a deep breath and says, "Thank God, what are you doing?"

I tell her I'm heading to the store to stock up on a few things since I'm working from home.

"Working from home? Does someone have corona at your school?"

"No, Mom. but we were just told that, to slow the spread, all schools are closed for at least two weeks to see what happens."

She says, "How is that going to work?"

"Mom, your guess is as good as mine."

"Where's Charlie?" she asks as if he is a child left alone at home.

"He's with me in the car, Mom, just relax," I say.

"I know, Lauren. There's just so much going on and I worry about you and your sister. Your father is out getting groceries and tissues. Make sure you get toilet paper; the news is saying that we may be locked down for weeks so you need to prepare."

Toilet paper was the least of my concerns. I was hoping all the Pino Noir wasn't gone. "Okay, I'll add tissues to my list." I go over the very few details my principal gave us and, just as I was running out of things to talk about, my mom interrupts me.

"Your sister is calling me, thank God. I was trying to reach her."

So happy that I have an out. I quickly tell her, "Check on Tab and to call me later."

She gave me a quick, "I love you and be safe," and ended the call.

I look over at Charlie, who has his head out the

window and pat him on his back. I say, "I'm glad you're the strong, silent type, LOL."

We pull into the parking lot which is jam packed. Cars for as far as the eyes could see. Holy moly, this is like a scene from a movie. I find a parking spot in the back of the parking lot, thinking this is part of my work out for today.

I crack the window enough for Charlie to get fresh air and give him a tight hug as if I will never return. He stares at me almost as if he's thinking the same. I walk away from the car and wish that I could take him with me but he's not a guide dog so that's a nope.

I enter the store with a pretty short grocery list since it's just Charlie and me. Tissues, wine, fruit, salad, shrimp and treats for Charlie. It's packed full of people but it is silent. That eerie silence as if the entire store was bracing for some type of impact. If someone were to drop a jar of pickles, the store would probably erupt into chaos.

"This is creepy," I say to myself as I swiftly move through the produce aisle. With the coronavirus, being at the store with everyone breathing made this visit a bit different from any other. After getting my items and noticing the tissue was down to only the generic brands, I am stuck with that but thinking how long could this actually last.

While waiting in line for almost twenty minutes, I think about Charlie in the car and wonder what he is doing. I saw on Instagram that this lady had a dog that would actually blow the car horn while she was inside any store. I would just die of embarrassment if Charlie would blow the car horn until I came out. That made me smile to myself in line. I hate when that happens; people often think that I'm talking to myself so I normally just nod and smile politely, hopefully letting them know that I'm not crazy.

I send a text to my mom letting her know that I'm almost out of the store. I wonder if Wade made it home okay. What about Simon? I hope he gets corona. Still no call or text and it has been weeks. I texted him last week to see if he wanted to get the few t-shirts he left at my house. Still waiting on the text to be read. It's been weeks at this point. I've moved on, just being polite and not giving him a reason to show up at my place unannounced. I'm officially single and on the market.

But the timing couldn't be worse. Who can date when there is a pandemic going around? I was looking forward to a Hot Girl Summer Part II which I wasn't apart of last year, because I was in a relationship with Simon the Asshole.

Based on the news, by the summer we should be in the clear. So, maybe, this will be perfect time for me to work on my squats so my ass will be a bit bigger this summer and to get in shape to find the man of my dreams.

These thoughts occupy my mind until I approach the self-checkout machine — which is a gift and a curse as it allows you very little interaction with people but the damn machine is so sensitive and annoying.

"Please place items in the bag," it shouts at me.

Duh, I know.

I leave the crowded store, set the bags on the back seat and enter the car.

It's now getting dark. The lights from the cars are

almost blinding as I turn out of the parking space. I make one more stop at Zoë's kitchen, wishing they had a drive through because, after standing in line for thirty minutes, I didn't want to get out of the car. Plus, I am too tired to cook the shrimp salad I had in mind for dinner. I am so tired. I am ready for wine, food, and bed.

Chapter 7

He pulls back the covers, awaking me from my sleep. I stir, not sure what or who is entering my bed. I don't have on any panties so whoever's face is heading down to my kitty is getting some very easy access. I feel the slow strokes of his tongue against the tip of my clitoris which makes me moan and arch my back. I have to know who this is.

I pull his sandy colored hair to get a glimpse of this person, and it's Wade. I knew that stroke felt familiar. I say his name confused on how he got here but not caring because it felt so good. He begins to lick until I am drenched and begging for him to enter me. I wait, anticipating his magic stick and, suddenly, the licking stops and he is gone.

I wake up, looking for him, but then realize I was dreaming. I roll over to Charlie lying next to me.

I quietly get out of bed, trying not to wake him, and walk into the living room. I grab the throw from the sofa and cover my bottom half, just in case Charlie walks into the living room. I slowly begin to massage my swollen clit with two fingers. No need to lick them because the dream had me wet enough to start a warm bath. I slowly rub my kitty and the fire feeling starts to rise. I slide one finger inside while keeping the other on my clit. I never knew my mother making me learn the piano would allow me to have great finger movement. I grab my breast with my free hand, letting it explore my hardened nipples.

I wish Wade was here because he is great at multitasking. I think of him finishing the dream, with him bending me over and taking me from behind. Each stroke harder than the last. I try to duplicate the pleasure with my fingers but they are not thick enough. They will have to do. I add another finger which causes my mouth to make the perfect O shape. I slide in and out slowly — the same way Wade would have done — until the fire becomes an explosion and I am left breathing hard and wanting more of the flames.

Just as I finish, I hear Charlie panting down the hallway. Like a person getting caught by their mother, I ball the cover up tight between my legs and tense up. I tell myself to relax. It's just Charlie. He jumps on the couch. I rub him with my dry hand and I stand up and tell him to stay while I clean up in the bathroom.

I felt so dirty that I opted for a shower. It was 3:15 a.m. I didn't have to report to work the next day so why not. I get in the shower and think about the dream, almost wanting to touch myself again.

"How did I get to that?" I ask myself. I then remember watching the Girlfriend Experience which turned me on way more than I had thought. My subconscious knew that I wanted Wade. Shit, I know that too. But it was Wade who had made the call to break things off until he knew what he wanted. Bullshit.

But he did send me a heart emoji earlier. Was that something or him just being concerned with the world coming to an end? Why would he send that? Wade is great at communicating. If he wanted to send a heart, why not give it to me officially? I'll take great care of it.

I watch the soap go down the drain right along with my hopes and dreams of wanting my dream man to want me again.

"What if I never got into a relationship with Simon? Maybe, we would have gotten back together by now," I tell myself.

I almost send him a text, telling him that I wanted him to come over and give me the live version of my dream but afraid of rejection, I decide not to. That's the thing, you never know what a person is thinking or what their intentions are. What if Wade's really a man whore but he just showed me this loving side to get what he wanted, only to string me along for years.

"I just wish..." I say out loud, not completing the sentence because I don't know what to wish for. Is it even fair to wish for the love of another one if the love is not reciprocated? I would almost be putting myself in the shoes of my mother, having a man stay with me just because I wished for it. Not only is that unfair to me, it's unfair to the man to be trapped with a woman because she made a wish.

The warm shower always brings the best thoughts out of me. I get my hormones and emotions in check when I think about what my mother said. It's only temporary. I have Charlie who is a protector, companion, and a loyal friend.

I get out the shower at 3:33 a.m. I put on a fresh white tee and my cheer shorts that I can still fit in. I check my ass in the mirror for plumpness and head to the living room with Charlie. We find Ridiculousness on TV, something that shouldn't start any fires between my legs.

Charlie lies on my legs this time. I feel his weight. "He's getting bigger," I tell myself. I curl up with my best friend and let the TV watch me on the couch, not knowing what the days ahead of me look like.

Chapter 8

It's day seven of quarantine and life is pretty great. I don't have to wake up at six a.m. any more which is amazing.

I had to tell Wade to stop calling at 6:45 a.m. He did it a few times just to hear my sleepy voice he said. He is flirting a lot lately. He felt bad for missing dinner last week so he promised tonight we will have dinner via zoom since we are both in lockdown with the rest of the world.

I wonder what I should wear. Wait, this isn't a date; this is what we usually do. Two friends/former lovers having dinner together. The only difference is that I'm single and so is he.

I pick up my coffee mug and head to the kitchen for my second cup of coffee. I'm watching the third hour of the Today Show. They're doing a cooking segment on chicken alfredo. Mental note to get alfredo and pasta from the grocery store.

Charlie looks at me from the couch, looking like he wants to join me but smart enough to know I'm coming back. Charlie and I have a very set schedule that we love. We wake at 8 a.m. and send out a morning message to the students and parents, letting them know the assignments for the day. The county gave each student their own personal computer. They are required to complete the work we send out each day and that's it. I usually send that while coffee is being made and after Charlie's morning walk. Since school is virtual, we just have to upload all the assignments for each week and check the work. If there are any questions, I set office hours for the parents to contact me. Besides the occasional grade level meeting which only last an hour, most of my day is free.

I head back to the sofa and tell Charlie to scoot over and get comfortable. I channel surf while he lies on my lap.

I see a text from Wade asking: what's for dinner? I told him to pick because I did last time but no Thai. I hate spicy food. He agrees and asked me if I had heard from Simon. I say no with the vomiting emoji to show my disgust at the thought of his name. I ask him why he wanted to know? There was a brief pause. Even though we were texting, it was as if we both felt that awkward silence while he was thinking of a reply. He finally says just asking. I waited that long for a just asking? I knew something was up because Wade didn't just ask questions. He quickly changed the subject and said that he couldn't wait for dinner because he needed to talk to me about something important but it had to be done in person.

"I smell BS, Charlie." He looks up me and I give him a kiss right on the mouth. I grab my phone to see what's trending on the social platforms and the first thing I see is Megan's countdown until her wedding. She even has a different dress for each marker and this is ninety-day dress and it was fabulous. What's the word for not jealous, but you are both happy for her yet wishing it was you. My subconscious yells out: hating! I roll my eyes, click the like button, and keep scrolling.

Giving myself a mental countdown of my own to finding a date, I wonder if Wade would take me. Should I ask? I wonder if their wedding will be affected by corona. So many questions with no answers.

I see a video that reminds me to get my squats in. I tell Charlie to join me. I listen to the video's workout mix and do my squats. Charlie watches me as my butt goes up and down. He walks around to get a sniff.

I laugh and tell him, "It's off-limits buddy," but he stays a bit longer before walking back to the couch as I finish.

"Phew, that was a good one, Charlie, we are going to have a Cardi B ass in no time," I look back and add, "Well, in due time."

I sit down to catch my breath. Charlie jumps on me, licking the little bit of sweat on my arms. "EWW," I yell, "you're gross."

I grab my phone and continue to scroll. I remember to text my sister about Charlie's zoom graduation. I decided to throw it this Saturday because I paid too much for his custom cap and gown for no one to see it. Plus, I want to celebrate his hard work completing obedience school. I tell her to please be on time and make sure Mom and Dad have the link. I will be busy setting up and I won't be able to help her. I will remind Wade tonight during our zoom call. I thought about inviting Simon, but decided not to. I mean, it's been almost a month and nothing.

I see that he finally read the text I sent about a week ago. I'm pretty sure that was just to clear the notification tab on the message icon. I mean, I know it was bad but was it that bad for him to just not talk to me and act like I never existed? We did spend three years together and had some great moments.

Like the time he surprised me with a trip to Savannah in December. It was beautiful, the giant Christmas tree in the center of the square. The custom ornaments we bought at the Antique Shoppe on the boardwalk and me laughing at him attempting to eat crab legs for the first time. There was a time when I thought Simon would potentially replace Wade and then there were times when I didn't want him to.

My sister texts back: Done, Done and Done. She was so doing much better and I was happy for her. I tell her thanks with an emoji. I check my email from work to make sure I didn't miss anything before my mid-morning nap.

"All clear, Charlie," I yell, "It's nap time." I grab the throw, wrap up and snuggle with Charlie with thoughts of Simon on my mind.

I wake up refreshed and ready for my zoom date with Wade. I'm so wondering what he has to tell me. I wonder what we're going to eat. Wade decided to order takeout from the same place and have it delivered to my house and his. He's so romantic. I am really hoping this is a prelude to us getting back together.

I take an extra-long bubble bath, nothing like a bath in the middle of the day. I take the time to even trim my kitty below, just in case he decides to come over in a passion of love for a taste. I curl my hair which is growing and getting healthier. The curls bounce perfectly as I lift them. I paint my nails and toes in Wade's favorite color

Auburn Orange. I wonder if he will notice.

I can't stop thinking about what wade wants to tell me. Is it good, bad, or ugly, What if he's getting engaged? I stop the overthinking train, on its tracks. My stomach growls a little, I check the time and see that it's almost five p.m time to get dressed.

What to wear? Charlie follows me into my walk-in closet that has a beautiful tiffany blue colored wall. One reason why I love this place. I pick out a cute, dark green maxi dress that complements my hazel eyes. Of course, I wear no bra and no panties just in case this becomes an X-rated dinner and a movie.

Just as I finish applying lotion and perfume, I hear Charlie bark and then the doorbell rang. I walk to the peephole to see the guy place the food and walk away. I guess this is what contactless delivery looks like. I hope Wade left a good tip.

As he enters the elevator, I open the door and grab the food. Italian, OMG, this man knows me so well. Plus, he got me extra bread sticks.

"Charlie, if you're good, I'll let you have one." He licks his chops as the smell of Chicken Parmesan fill the air. With my mom being half Greek and Italian, I always grew up eating the best foods. This wasn't my mom's but it was the next best thing.

I go to the kitchen and only put half the portion of food on the plate. I don't want Wade to think I am getting fat now, do we? Charlie and I share a bread stick. I put just one on my plate with some of the salad in a small silver bowl and place it on my desk.

I open my computer and check my email and I see

the link from Wade. I'm so excited. I rush back to the kitchen to grab my wine. With Charlie on my heels, he almost trips me.

"Charlie," I yell, "watch it big guy." I get back to my chair to do one more hair and makeup check in the computer monitor and clicked the link. The computer is checking the audio and tells me to wait while the host is preparing the meeting. I hold up my glass of wine and strike a cute little pose, hoping he notices all the effort I put in for this evening. When Wade appears on the screen, what I saw almost made me drop my glass of wine.

Chapter 9

"Why are you in your truck?" I ask before he can even say anything.

"I know, L.A., this is not what I was expecting either but I have some news," he says. "Definitely not what I wanted to tell you, but my mom called this afternoon and told me that my dad has the coronavirus."

"Oh my God, Wade, I'm so sorry. How is he doing?"

"Well, right now, he's hanging in there. They are hoping to get him on a ventilator by the end of the week. That's if there are any available."

"So, you're driving to North Carolina?"

"Yeah, my parents live right outside of Durham. I left around two so I should get there around seven," he says.

I ask, "How are you feeling?"

He says, "L.A., I don't know. I'm numb right now. I just want to get to my mom and makes sure she's okay. My dad is a fighter, I think he will be fine. My mom is scared and doesn't know what to do. I'm just glad I convinced them not to move back to San Diego." Wade's parents moved two years ago to get away from the busy city of Atlanta to a smaller town near Durham, North Carolina. "I would have hated to drive across the country but would have done it."

"Not alone," I yell out, "I wish I could have come

with you."

"I know, L.A., I would have loved that and, believe me, I thought about it but, with all the restrictions at the hospital and me possibly having to quarantine two weeks before I can even go see my dad, we would be stuck in the house." I thought about being in quarantine with Wade. Oh, what a quarantine that would be. Wade's voice brought me back from horny land and back to the severity of the situation at hand.

I just quietly reply, "You're right."

"Enough about that," he says, "did you get your favorite food?"

"Yes," I say, "thank you, Wade, you know me so well." I almost say I love you but catch myself and say, "I hate that we can't eat together."

He laughs, holds up a breadstick and waves it at the camera. Wade's sat high in his big F-150 Blue and Orange truck. He has the phone mounted on his dash and chomps on the breadstick. "I said we were having dinner together and I meant that," he says.

"What could you possibly be eating whilst driving?"

"I got a sausage and pepper Stromboli with fried calamari on the side and, of course, you know the meals come with salad and breadsticks."

"But I have something that you don't," I tell him. I hold up the bottle of Meomi.

"That's my favorite," he says and follows with, "Oh my, what do we have here?" he says, "I love the nail color, Madam," using the worse French accent I've ever heard which makes me almost spit out my wine.

"You are such a clown," I say.

He says, "You like it."

As a matter of fact, I love you is what I wanted to say but I just went with the simple, "Whatever."

We laugh and joke telling each other about our days and even share stories and shared memories pretty much until he got to his parent's house.

"Well, L.A., this is my exit," he tells me.

"Thanks, Wade, for an amazing evening. This has been the best date I've had in forever." This makes me think of Simon, ugh.

"You're welcome, L.A. I look forward to many more, Lauren," he says.

"Hey, what did you have to tell me?" I ask him before he ends the video call.

"Well, L.A., I don't know what this road with my parents will take me, but I will tell you in due time, I promise."

I say, "Okay," giving him a pouty lip.

He smiles and says, "In due time." And ends the call.

Chapter 10

I'm so in love with Wade, more than ever before. I don't know if it's the month of being alone, not being hugged, touched, or kissed by a man, but I miss him badly.

"This is sad" I say and I get up and stretch not realizing we had been on the call for two hours. I notice Charlie standing by the door. "I'm so sorry Charlie it's time for your walk."

We head out of the building and my mind is trying its best to figure out what exactly Wade wanted to say. Could it be that he wants to get back together? Or will he propose? So many questions and scenarios.

I stop thinking about us and start to think about his parents. This virus has already killed so many people and the elderly are not bouncing back like the others after two weeks of quarantine. I pray they are okay.

I see a neighbor also walking her dog. We wave and barley speak, almost as if we have the virus.

"This thing is making everyone crazy," I say to Charlie. He seems excited about being outside and ignores my comment. "Typical man," I tell him.

We get back in the house and here comes the silence. I like living alone but, damn, it's lonely. I like not having to argue with Simon about what we're having for dinner, because he didn't like what I picked or watched on tv. But it was some type of communication. How did we last three years? It went by so fast.

I go to the kitchen to get a bottle of water and find my way to the couch. I take off my sweats to let Ms Kitty breathe. It gets hot down there, especially since Wade did all that flirting just to leave a girl hot and bothered. I felt warmth between my thighs as if someone was working hard to start a campfire with only two sticks.

I turn on my show The Girlfriend Experience which is pretty racy and gets me turned on. Maybe because the actress looks a bit like me — except I may weigh a little more and I for sure have a bigger butt than she does. All it takes is one episode for the fire to start but there's no need to call the fire department. Watching her have sex and be free is something I admire about the character. She is living her truth and no one is going to stop her.

I head to the bedroom, while Charlie is asleep on the couch. I head to my trunk to pick out the right tools for the fire and I go with the dildo. I apply a small amount of lube just in case Ms Kitty is tight. It has been a while. I slide it in and, like that the dildo inside feels amazing. Almost as thick as wade I am so wet. I am so wet, the dildo inside feels amazing. Almost as thick as Wade. I wish he was here. Thinking of him makes me push it in a little deeper, just the way he would do. Taking me to the edge but never dropping me. I make every stroke last as long as it can, only to repeat, not wanting it to end.

My arms get tired, so I straddle my invisible man. I sit on it and it touches my soul. I make a soft moan as I rotate my hips around the tip. I start bouncing which causes my breasts to do a dance as well. I grab them softly, squeezing my nipples which makes me wetter. It sounds like I'm stirring a pot of spaghetti.

I feel the orgasm rushing like a tsunami.

I scream out: "Wade! Oh, Wade, I'm coming." I almost lift completely off the bed from how hard I had cum. I roll over to my side to catch my breath and to find the towel I had grabbed. I find it and lie on my back and place the towel between my legs. I catch my breath and sit up, only to see Charlie sitting at the door.

I startle because I really forgot he was in the house. Did he just see me have an orgasm? I was so loud. I feel so embarrassed.

"He's a dog. Who is he going to tell? He doesn't even know what's going on," I tell myself. If the girl from the show can have sex for cash with strangers, I can masturbate in front of my dog. So instead of wrapping up with a blanket, I walk proudly past Charlie to the bathroom for clean-up.

I come back to bed and I grab my phone. I text Wade:

Thanks again for another wonderful evening.

I wish he knew about the last part.

I pray your dad gets well soon and tell your mom hi for me.

I also tell him that if he can't make Charlie's virtual graduation it was fine. In fact, I insisted that he didn't come and to focus on his dad's health. He quickly likes the message.

I lay in bed thinking about the first time I met his dad. We got off the bus from Junior high and his dad was under the hood of the car changing something. I remember thinking he looks exactly like Wade but he had a salt and pepper beard which made him even more attractive. His dad told him to get ready for baseball practice and asked who I was.

Wade smiled and said, "A friend."

He laughed, stuck out his oily hand and said, "Hi, friend. Do you have a name?"

I shyly said, "Yes, Lauren Peterson." I shook his oily hand.

"Well, I'm Alon Jameson but everyone calls me A.J. You're not afraid of getting dirty I see" he replied as I held is oily, greasy hand. "Wade, she's a keeper."

"Dad, stop it," he yelled as he ran off.

I said my goodbyes and walked the rest of the way home.

I say a silent prayer that his father beats this virus and drift off to sleep.

Chapter 11

I wake up early, around 7 a.m. to make sure the PowerPoint presentation I created for Charlie's graduation was completed. I only had to add some music and a few for photos for it to be worthy for my family but mostly for Instagram. If it wasn't for Charlie, I would be so alone. God forbid, my mom or dad get corona, I would be devastated.

I think about Wade who is an only child and him probably being just as alone as I am.

With clubs, bars, and any place you typically would go to meet someone being closed, I couldn't even find a date if I wanted to. I have never liked the whole online dating thing and there is no way I'm meeting a stranger who might have corona. So, at this point, I may be single forever.

I watch the final presentation one last time to make sure it is perfect and it makes me smile.

I get my cup of coffee as the last drip enters the mug and I enter my bedroom to see Charlie snuggled up on what is now his side of the bed. For once, I'm glad Simon didn't listen to me when I told him I didn't want a dog because, if he had, I wouldn't have Charlie during the loneliest time of my life.

"Okay, Charlie, it's show time," I say as I adjust his

cap and smooth the wrinkles out of his gown.

I wait as everyone enters the zoom meeting. I see my mom and dad appear. I wave.

My mom says, "Oh, how adorable Charlie looks in his blue cap and gown." My dad just nods in agreeance.

Tabitha shows up one minute late, probably because she helped my parents. She also loves Charlie's outfit so I decide to spare her feelings about her tardiness.

Just as I was about to start the ceremony, I see Wade's name enter on the screen. I pause, hoping that it is not a dream.

"Wade!" I shout out, "What are you doing on here?" I try to hide my excitement.

"Hi, everyone," he says before he answers me. They all speak. My mom smiles and claps as if no one can see her.

"Mom," I whisper.

"I know this was important to you and I love Charlie and I wouldn't miss it," Wade says.

Seeing him at his parent's home makes me want to be with him. I know how much he loved his parents, especially his dad. For him to show up while his dad is in the hospital, is major and I know he is going to be my husband. I just have to wait for him to ask.

I begin to feel the fire that often leads me to my bedroom but I fight off the desire to focus on the task at hand.

I start the ceremony with a short speech about Charlie and how he became a part of my life, making sure to leave Simon's name out of it just in case Wade thought we were getting back together. The presentation has tons of pictures of Charlie at obedience school — with all of his trainers and the other dogs he had become fond of. It is like a dog's senior year of high school, if you could imagine, full of good times and great memories.

I present Charlie with his certificate, which the school emailed a few days after telling us about the postponing of the graduation, and a giant bone I bought when I picked up his cap and gown. It is wrapped in a bow and Charlie is so excited which gave me a chance to show off his skills.

"Sit," I say. He sits. "Down, good boy, now roll over, sit up, shake and jump."

My parents, Wade, and even Tabitha are all impressed on how well he listened to me.

I brag and say, "He has more tricks that he does when he's outdoors." They all applaud and I say, "I now present to you, from your graduating class of 2020 from Roof Dog Academy, Charlie Peterson."

Wade stands and my dad he even claps and smiles. It warms my heart being this close to my family even though we are so far apart. I end the call, hoping Wade would stay on and he does.

I ask, "How is your dad doing?"

He says, "He's stable; we're just waiting for them to get a ventilator here. The hospital will only let one person in at a time. So, my mom and I agreed that she would do the day shift and I would do the night."

"I'm so sorry, Wade. I know your dad is going to get better."

"I hope you're right, L.A. It's just, with all the news reports of the death toll rising every day, it's like my dad has no chance, he's waiting in line to die."

"Stop it," I say, "We're not thinking like that, positive thoughts only."

Seeing Wade weak and vulnerable like this doesn't sit right with me. He is always so strong and confident, just like his dad.

"Wade," I ask, "Would you like for me to come and stay with you during the day to keep you company?"

He looks at the screen, as if he wants to say yes and I would be there in a moment's notice. I sit at the edge of my seat waiting for him to reply.

He puts his head down and says, "Sorry, L.A., I can't risk exposing you to corona. People at this hospital are dying left and right. It's so packed that it took me forty-five minutes to find a parking space. If something happened to you, I would never forgive myself."

I nod quietly, almost in tears because Wade was starting to cry.

"I have to go run some errands for my mom; there is nothing to eat and I'm starved. Can we chat later?" he asks.

"Only if you're up to it," I tell him.

"Okay," he says. I want to tell him that I love him so bad, but his voice interrupts my thoughts when he says, "Thanks for always being here, L.A. I really appreciate you."

"It's nothing," I say. "You're my best friend."

He smiles and says, "Thanks," and, just as quickly as he appeared, he is gone.

Charlie and I clean up from the graduation celebration. I think I went a bit overboard with the confetti.

I change out of my all-black dress, and red heels, which I don't think anyone noticed, into sweats, a sweatshirt and comfortable shoes.

I need to get out the house, with all the emotions I am feeling about Wade and his dad. I need an out.

Charlie and I decide to go to Target which hasn't closed, thank God for essential workers. I go and pick up the last do it at home nail kit that I saw on Tik-Tok. I guess everyone saw it based on how the beauty department area is bare. The Starbucks inside is closed which sucks so no fancy drink for me. I head down just about every aisle in the store so I don't have to go back home to the silence.

I then remember Charlie is in the car and he might start blowing the horn. LOL. I'm so silly, I remind myself.

I see masks in the store so I grab a pack. I see a few people in the store wearing them but, for the most part, most people aren't. I guess they are following Trump who said that he wasn't going to wear one. I heard that on the news this morning.

I pick up a few grocery items, mostly junk food but a few healthy snacks as well. I head to checkout and I notice all the stickers on the floor directing you where to go and to social distance. I overhear a couple talking about how this is like the movie Contagion on Netflix. I take a mental note of that and head out to the car with my evening planned.

I grab the popcorn from the microwave and dump it into my large, silver bowl. I taste one for a quality check and it's perfect.

I say, "Everyone says this movie tells the story of what will possibly happen with corona."

Charlie looks up as if he understands me. I pour my second glass of wine, feeling like Olivia Pope. I had thought about asking Wade to watch with me, but, with the current state of his dad, this movie is too close to home.

I sent him a text to check on him a few hours ago, still no response. He's probably busy with so many things.

Charlie is in his permanent spot on the couch which is his head on my lap. I feed him a few pieces of popcorn; it wouldn't be fair not so share with my date since no man on Earth wants me. I tell myself to relax and start the movie, thinking how much better this would be if Wade was here instead of me experiencing the real-life version of the movie alone.

Chapter 12

The days of quarantine were fun in the beginning. The first three weeks were amazing. I was able to catch up on all my lesson plans for the rest of the year. We only had a few weeks to go, anyway, and not to forget being out for spring break. I had an amazing trip planned to ski in Colorado for the first time. It was going to be a girl's trip with some teachers from my school and another elementary school in the area.

That all came to an abrupt stop when COVID-19, newly named. hit the scene.

I've done a great job of keeping busy by organizing my closet, donating some items and working out. This is all an effort to not be sad because of how lonely I am.

I've had Charlie and he is great but I need that touch from a warm body. Wade has been a bit harder to get in contact with since they moved his dad to hospice two weeks ago. Wade hasn't been the same and this has taken a lot out of him. The strong man I once knew is starting to vanish along with his father. Each time we talk, I can hear the pain and anguish in his voice and it's heartbreaking because there is nothing that I can do to help.

I also wanted to bring up what he had to tell me during our canceled dinner. I don't because that would just seem so selfish but… UGH.

I scream into the pillow on my bed. I only got out of bed this morning to walk Charlie and since then, I climbed back in bed and haven't moved. I don't even know what day of the week it is.

I grab my phone to check the calendar and I see that I have four missed calls from Wade. I then remember how I put my phone on silent last night while watching a movie to enhance the experience.

UGH, I am so mad at myself.

I quickly change the setting to ring from vibrate and call Wade. The phone seems to ring forever and on the last ring I hear a sad "Hello." I can hear his mother in the background crying. I know immediately what has happened.

"Wade, I'm so sorry," I say. He just holds the phone, quietly sobbing. "I'm coming to see you, Wade. I'm getting dressed right now."

I move toward my closet and I finally hear his voice, first cracking but then strong, he says a loud, "No!" This leaves me shocked because Wade has never raised his voice, especially at me. The only time I've heard Wade yell was at a baseball game during his senior year when he punched the pitcher for hitting him with a pitch.

I stand in my bedroom with tears in my eyes, not knowing if I am crying because of the rejection or because his father has passed.

I ask, "Why not?"

He says, "Lauren, my mom and I both have COVID or corona, or whatever the hell you want to call this fucking virus." He was yelling by the end. He calms down and sadly whispers, "I have to bury my father and we can't even have a funeral because of social distancing."

I start to cry with him. "So, I can't come and see you?" I ask like a child.

"No, L.A., it's not safe. I'm not safe. I would hate to give you this virus. My mom and I are going to quarantine in the house. I'm really afraid my mom won't have the strength to fight now that my dad is gone."

"She will, Wade, you just have to stay strong for the both of you."

"I will be fine. I've had it for a few days now and I'm feeling myself bounce back."

That makes me smile. "That's great," I tell him. "But what about your mom?"

"She seems to be getting better but, with the news of my father passing this morning, I don't know how her body is going to handle it."

Wade and I talk a few more minutes, with him beginning to ask how I was doing during quarantine. I told him I am lonely but Charlie is taking good care of me and that I am staying busy with cleaning, organizing. I even told him about my adventure to goodwill when all of the clothes I had neatly folded fell when the guy picked up the bag and, because it was so heavy, he fell along with all the clothes to the floor. He laughed a bit which made me feel like there would be a rainbow at the end of the tunnel almost bringing me out my pity party.

Then, he says, "I love you, Lauren."

I say, "I love you too, Wade," and we hang up.

Wait was that a 'I love you, I love you'? Or a

'because my father died, I love everyone, I love you'? I am so confused. I have so many questions.

I check my phone for the time. Maybe I should call Tabitha; she's up it 8:45 a.m. What else is she doing? I call Tabs and she answers on the third ring.

"Are you up?" I ask.

"I am now, little sis," she says jokingly.

I tell her the sad details of Wade's father passing away. Tabitha sheds a few tears because we all saw and felt the love that Wade and his father, Alan, shared with each other. It is like watching someone not only lose their dad but their best friend. I then bring up the part I really called about which was do determine which; I love you; he meant. We analyze the phrase in every way possible.

"First," she asks, "Was it on zoom? Could you see his face?"

I say, "No."

Then, she asks others questions but the answers aren't clear and everything is still up in the air.

"Well, Lauren, I guess you're going to have to just wait and see what happens. You can never tell what a person's true intentions are. That's the hardest thing about letting people in your life. They may seem genuine and say all the right things but you never know what they feel on the inside. You really have to wait and see how the relationship plays out."

Tabitha sounds like a woman that was divorced and has been through some things because that is the best advice I have heard. I tell her that and she continues with saying how therapy has been amazing for her even though she was attending virtually. We talk a few minutes more until we both end the call to have breakfast.

As I sit and eat my bagel and blueberries on the couch, I look at the dining room table I bought three years ago, thinking that I would have a family by now. What a waste. I am thinking about selling it and getting a peloton. Me having a tight fit body might help fill this place up with kids?

The sun is shining bright through the curtains.

"Charlie, you want to go for a hike today?" He sits up and his tail begins to wag. "I need to clear my head," I tell myself.

After a shower, I change into a cute workout outfit I had bought online since walking has become my new hobby.

Charlie and I head up to Kennesaw to walk the mountain trail. It is warmer outside so I am excited to feel the warm sun on my skin. I haven't been able to get to a tanning salon in weeks and I need as much vitamin D as possible.

Speaking of D, I really need sex. Even though Simon is a jerk, he was decent in bed but I can never get that desperate. I find myself wanting it more than ever. I think the fact that I'm home most of the day half naked and everything on TV, Instagram, and Tik-Tok is so sexual, not to mention me having to take a break from the Girlfriend experience. That show turns me on so much. But tonight, I am watching and can't wait.

Charlie and I had an amazing walk. The trail is pretty busy. There are some cute guys who just admire me with their eyes but say nothing. It's difficult to bring someone home to a hook up when you're not sure if they have

Covid or not.

Charlie and I take great pictures which I post on all social media accounts. This should get the likes going, I tell myself.

I even got a like from Wade. He is amazing even with everything going on he still finds time for me. Why can't he just ask me to be his girlfriend again, or better yet, his wife?

We get home. I give Charlie the biggest bowl of water because it's kind of hard to let a dog drink from a water bottle without wasting half of it. Next time, bring water dish; I make a mental note.

I shower again to get the sweat and dirt off of me. I get out the shower and I feel great but my legs feel tight from the hike. I turn to the side and see my glutes and they are nice, tight and, most importantly, growing.

"In due time," I say, "LOL."

I squeeze my breasts and they bounce back in to place as I let them go. My nipples begin to get hard as the warm air from the steam begins to cool. It's late in the afternoon and I feel the fire begin to start but I control it. "Later."

I slip on my t-shirt and grab my laptop to grade some work from my students. I start working from the desk but move to the couch because Charlie looks so alone. The work the students turn in online, is so much easier to grade, rather than worksheets that I have to keep track of and send home each week in the kids' daily folder.

Being a teacher in 2020 is good so far but I do miss the kids laughing and playing, especially the girls — they have the biggest fights over who's friends with who. I could start a day time talk show based on their drama. Thinking of them makes me want to have kids again. The dining room table almost seems to mocking me as it still sits their empty.

"I'm getting a peloton," I say just as the commercial appears for the fourth time during whatever Charlie was watching.

After about two straight hours of working, I'm all caught up. I send an email to my grade level lead teacher.

Time for food. I make a shrimp salad with all the fixings — tomatoes, cucumbers, crotons, cheese — and it tastes amazing. I put a few grape tomatoes in Charlie's dish and he seems to like them. Well, he seems to like anything I put in front of him.

I call my mom after dinner to share the news of Wade's dad and she is devastated. It hits close to home because my dad and Alon were the same age. My dad, fifty-seven, is older than my mom, fifty-one. My mother tells me how sorry she is. She asks for the address to send flowers to his family. I send the information.

I don't bring up that Wade said he loved me because I don't think my mother would understand. I don't think she even knows what real love is.

She tells me to be safe and to follow all of the CDC guidelines. I agree and tell her to do the same. We say our goodbyes and hang-up.

Chapter 13

It's late, around 11 p.m. and I can't sleep so I look online for a peloton and decide not to make an impulse purchase.

I know my family is coming. I just have to get Wade through this and we will be back on track.

I get comfy on the couch and begin watching the first few minutes of The Girlfriend Experience. It's the episode where she sets up video cameras to watch herself masturbate. I am so turned on.

I had thought, if I had a distraction like a bowl of ice cream and if I watched next to Charlie, that it would help control the flames. I pick up the spoon and put it to my mouth, not realizing that it's melting and some drips onto my thigh.

Watching her watch herself makes the fires roar like the ones in California. I close my eyes as I imagine I am there with her. I spread my legs to let the fire breathe but we all know that makes the fire grow even faster.

I feel Charlie beginning to lick the ice cream from my thigh. I don't stop him. It feels amazing. The tackiness of his tongue on my thigh makes this feel like foreplay. I rub my clit as I grab the spoon to put more ice cream on my thigh for him to lick.

While I play with my swollen clit, I moan. As Charlie licks, I flick and flick until I explode, causing Charlie to jump off the couch.

As I open my eyes, I feel as naked as Eve did in the garden with the snake.

What did I just do?

I try to ignore the endorphins my body is giving me, that let me know that Mrs Kitty was pleased with the performance. But my thoughts were all over the place.

Did I just have sex with... No, no, no. He only licked my thigh.

But as I began to judge myself, I hear the chick from the show telling her sister: "So what if I have sex with people for money? It's my life."

In this moment, I feel the same way. No one has to know about what I did in my house with my dog. Besides, he only licked my thigh.

I clean up my mess and I head to bed with Charlie on my heels.

I wake up feeling refreshed and energized. The hike yesterday really drained me and I needed all of the sleep. I don't remember falling asleep up until I see Charlie lying in bed and I remember him on my inner thigh.

I close my eyes and shake the memory away as I tell myself nothing happened.

I call Charlie's name to take him for his morning walk. Charlie does his morning business and we head back into the house.

My phone rings from the bedroom as we walk in. I rush to get it and trip over Charlie's leash, almost causing me to fall.

"Charlie," I say, I don't know if I am irritable at him for last night or for making me trip?

I get to the phone, and it's Wade. I then remember the text I sent him before watching The Girlfriend Experience, hoping he would call during the show and help me finish what I had already started but he didn't.

I pick up, sounding a bit winded from my stumble and Wade being so attentive asked if I am okay.

I tell him, "It's just Charlie in the way."

He jokes, "You guys are having too much fun over there."

I say shyly, "Yeah," whilst I think about last night's fun and quickly change the subject. "So how are you and your mom doing?"

"It's only been a day, and my mom is taking it bad. So am I," he says, "but I'm trying to be strong for her. I need her to get better. I can't have her die from this thing too." He tells me about the plans for burial.

I ask, "Is there any way I can come see you?"

Wade is dead set on not seeing me until this thing is over. "L.A., I can't risk it. I've been wearing masks and washing my hands and I have no idea how I tested positive." I really hope he changes the subject to us, I tell myself. Wade, as if he read my mind, says, "I really appreciate you, L.A., for being here for me. I have no siblings and not much family but talking to you makes it feel like I have all of that, plus more."

I blush and say, "Aww, that's sweet," and remind him that I was and still am his girl.

He says, "I know but you've been stuck in a relationship for the past three years while I'm out here single."

"Wait, you weren't in a relationship with any other

73

girl since we broke up?" I ask.

He laughs, "If you call one-night stands and hook-ups relationships, sure. That was then but I have not done that in a year and a half. That bachelor life is cool but it gets old fast."

"I had no clue," I say. "I thought you were in a relationship and just decided to keep the women a secret from me — that's why I stayed with Simon so long, waiting on you."

"Wait, you only were with Simon to pass the time?" he asks.

"Yes, Wade."

As I am about to go over the breakup that he caused, I hear his mother coughing in the background.

He tells me to hold on. He comes back about thirty seconds later and says, "I have to call you back."

"I say, "Okay," and, just as I was about to say my I love you, the phone call ends.

What the fuck? How did he not know that? I mean, we were in an entire relationship and he breaks it off. If he never would have done that, we could be married by now with kids.

I hate men. They are so dumb and clueless.

I mean, was it me? Did I make Wade think that I didn't want him any more? I guess I did. I did have a boyfriend who stayed over about three times a week.

But by the way I complained to Wade about the relationship with Simon, I thought he would have known I was unhappy and wanted him.

I pace the floor, trying to gather all of my thoughts.

I make a cup of coffee and immediately regret it. I should have made tea. Now I'm questioning all of my decisions.

I think about calling Tabitha but decide to wait since I've already called her twice this week before noon. Plus, it is Saturday and she might be sleeping in.

I grab my coffee and a banana and sit on the couch. Charlie joins me. I rub his head and thanks him for being so loyal. I wish all men could go to obedience school and be taught how to listen to women. The only time me and Charlie have an issue is when he wants to be too close to me and ends up tripping me. Now, what woman wouldn't want their man near them at all times?

I start to regret even bringing the conversation up. I mean, what did he think I was going to do? Charlie just sits and wait by the phone until he got his rocks off with God knows who. Charlie looks up at me confused but stays near me.

I hope his mom is okay. I'm so selfish. His mom is fighting for her life and I'm getting upset over an unfinished conversation.

I open my messages and begin to type: 'Wade, you have always been my first love. From the day I saw your family move in I just knew I had to know you. I know this is out the blue, but I feel like I need to tell you how I feel. If you ever doubted my love for you, I want to let it be known that I want to be with you and only you. I know there's Simon but he's a small blip in my life. I know you have to be with your mom. So, call me when you have time. I pray she gets well soon.' I add an orange and blue heart emoji and send.

I sit the phone down and decide to take a nap. It is too early for this much emotional distress.

Chapter 14

Days turn into weeks, and weeks into months. It's now June and I haven't heard from Wade.

Charlie and I are closer than ever.

The first few days I was really worried because he did leave the call because his mother was sick battling Covid so I thought the worst.

The fourth day was when I was over Wade. He finally read the message but did not respond. I was livid. How could I just pour my heart out to this guy who I thought loved me and he not even respond? I guess Wade isn't the great communicator I thought he was.

The next mistake I did was tell my mother what happened. Now every day she asks, "Have you heard from Wade?" I finally told her yesterday to please stop asking about him. She was offended but at least she knows how I feel.

My sister told me to relax and that he had a lot going on and that I was being spoiled and self-centered as usual. I agreed that she was right and I decided not to communicate with Wade until he was ready and I did just that.

Corona has not gone anywhere but things here in Atlanta are opening back up. Clubs, bars and restaurants are open and the city is coming back to life. I am a bit nervous about going around strangers. I haven't been on any dates, besides the one's Charlie and I have at home. I just don't know how to interact with people whose face I can't see. All I see are eyes, no cute smiles, or white teeth, just eyes. I need a change of scenery.

Two months ago, Megan posted that she was having her wedding but it was going to be smaller. I guess I was close enough to Megan and made the cut of the 75 people that would be there and decided to go.

The wedding is in Destin, Florida and Charlie and I are hitting the road. All of the bags sat in the living room packed. I looked over the checklist for Charlie and I was happy with all that I had accomplished.

"OK, Charlie, we leave at 10a.m. tomorrow morning."

It was around 8pm and I went to run a long hot bath with bubbles to relax my body from all the moving around Charlie and I did today.

I pour my second glass of wine to get my body warm for the night ahead. I get out and dry off my body. I head to my trunk and take out my magic wand and dildo.

Make sure I pack these, I tell myself.

I crawl on to the bed and I start the first fire with the wand. I move it in a circular motion causing my body shivers as if I was left in the cold.

In between breaths, I call Charlie into the room. He enters and I tell him to sit. I rotate my hips harder on the wand making the intensity even more pleasurable. Charlie watched as I please myself at the foot of the bed.

I say, "Up." He jumps onto the bed.

I grab the dildo and insert it — well, as much of it as

I could take.

I move the wand and I give Charlie the command to lick as I point at my wet vagina. His thick warm tongue begins to work magic on my clitoris and having the dildo inside made it feel like I was having a threesome. His licks are strong and fast, just how I like it. He bumps the dildo, making it go even deeper which causes me to arch my back. I feel the climax coming.

I remind myself not to scream his name like the time before. I can't let the neighbors hear me. I cum so hard in just a matter of minutes.

I give the command of stop and down and Charlie does just that and lays on the floor. Within in moments, I am fast asleep.

Chapter 15

"It's vacation day," I shout to Charlie, rubbing his face as I wake up. "Let's hit the road buddy."

I get up, start my coffee and take Charlie out for his morning walk.

We come in and I text my mom and sister the address of the hotel and also make sure they both have my location shared on their phones.

I make a small breakfast of pancakes and fruit.

While cleaning up, I hear noise from the parking lot. Horns blowing and people yelling.

"What is going on Charlie?" I ask. "Must be people getting in their cars for the first time and forgetting how to drive," I joke.

I begin to grab bags and then Charlie starts barking. "Not you too, buddy," I say. "The cars got you fussy this morning."

Just then there is a knock on the door. "Who could this be?" I say.

I look through the peep hole to see who this unannounced visitor is. I see eyes and mask and a beard and it looks like no one I know.

I ask, "Can I help you?" I'm mad at myself; I should have said nothing.

The voice says, "It's me?"

"Who is me?" I yell. "I'm going to call the police."

The masked man removes his mask and I saw the lips. The lips of Wade who is an excellent kisser.

I open the door and he's standing there. Not looking like the strong former baseball player, I knew.

I hug him, feeling how much weight he's lost.

"Where have you been? What are you doing here?" With all my questions and excitement of seeing Wade, I didn't even realize that Charlie is barking and is trying to attack Wade. "Down, Charlie," I yell telling him to sit on his chair.

He hesitates for the first time since obedience school and I am shocked.

"Wade jokes and says, "Well, it has been a while since I've seen you too. Plus, with this beard, it may be hard to recognize me."

We walk over to the sofa, Charlie not once taking his eyes off of Wade. It makes me a bit nervous.

We sit and I say, "OK, sir, please talk."

"Where do I start?" Wade says. "Lauren, my mom passed."

I drop my keys and shades and gave him a hug with tears swelling in my eyes. I tell him how sorry I am. I feel miserable for ignoring him and not reaching out.

He told me that it was his fault. "In fact, your message is what kept me going. After we got off the phone that day, Mom's fever spiked to a hundred and four and I had to get her to the emergency room. I was in such a rush that I left my phone at home. My mom passed four days later. I sat in the hospital for hours until I was able to drive back to their house. I didn't want to face their things alone. I wanted to end it all but, knowing that you loved me, I couldn't be weak, to take my life and allow you to feel the pain that I felt losing both my parents."

I am stunned. "So, what are you saying, Wade?" I ask.

He says, "I want you and I to be us again."

I am so happy. It feels as if this is a dream.

He notices that I have bags packed. "Where are you going?" he asks

"I was heading to Destin with Charlie for Megan's wedding this weekend. You caught me just as I was about to leave."

"I guess this was destiny," he says. He tells me that he has so much more to tell me but, as soon as he got back to the city, I was the first person he wanted to see. "I want to see you as soon as you get back," he tells me. "I want to talk to you about something."

"Is it what I think it is?" I ask.

"Maybe," he says. "I have to check on my place and go by the office. I haven't been there in months."

We walk to the door and, as he exits, Wade turns and gives me the most passionate kiss I have had in years. I couldn't even enjoy it long enough because Charlie begins to bark like he is going to attack Wade.

"Down, boy," I yell, "sit and stay."

Charlie backs away into his corner.

Wade laughs and says, "Well, I guess I got to show the king that there is a new sheriff in town."

I laugh nervously as he pecks me on the lips and heads out and tells me to drive safely.

Chapter 16

"Charlie, how could you act like that?" I say to him in the car. I am so embarrassed. "What has gotten into you?"

Then it hits me. What if Charlie is jealous? I mean we do spend a lot of quality time together. Especially since I hadn't heard from Wade for the past two months. "Charlie are you jealous?" I ask him as if he is going to reply.

He just stares at me from the backseat. I didn't let the window down, forcing him to hear me fuss over his behavior.

It reminds me of the times my mom would do that with me. She would plan long drives and ask about boys and sex. The car was the perfect place because I couldn't walk away or pretend the TV was too loud and ignore her.

That's where I told her that Wade was my first. She was a bit disappointed that I was only seventeen but I thought that was an accomplishment, considering I knew girls that were fourteen when they lost their virginity.

I guess it was just mother's intuition because she asked me to go to Target with her and I was like 'sure' so I jumped in the car expectantly, not knowing it was an ambush.

She started off with just simple stuff, so off topic that I wouldn't even expect. My mom was so into pop culture.

She knew who was dating who in Hollywood and all the inside tips on what was going on.

She went from that to "So have you and Wade had sex yet?"

I was so shocked that all I could do was say "Yes." It didn't help that it happened three days ago and was fresh in my mind. I was actually thinking about it when she asked. My mom had been so open about sex and me exploring myself. I guess she had to do it because my dad didn't seem like the foreplay type. We talked openly about sex toys and what to use for what and how to keep them clean and sanitized.

As I got older, I didn't talk about my sex life much with my mom because she equipped me with all the tools I needed.

I wonder if I could tell her this.

The ride to Destin was smooth. I get there right at five hours. I pull into the hotel, check in and get ready for my bath.

I face time Wade from the bed. I should have brought my mac book so I could have given him a real show without having to hold my phone, just in case it goes in that direction. We talk for about four hours on the phone, him telling me the sad details of his mother's death. How he was the only person at the burial site.

I ask, "Why didn't you call me?"

He just says, "I needed the time alone to truly heal. Wade explains it all for me. He says, "If I would have used you as a decoy to hide the pain, hurt, and grief, I would have just bottled them up and never healed." He spent most of the days just crying.

Hearing him say that made me feel so bad. I should have been there for him.

"I was in their home," he continued, "with all their things they had collected over the years. Old photographs and love letters written by both my parents. They even kept all the cards they had given each other over the years. I read them all. Every day, over and over, listening to their voices and how they expressed their love for each other. That all made me think of you. It was as if their death is what brought me to you. I never thought I would be good enough for you, L.A. I was scared that I would marry you and fail at being a husband. I thought that dating these other women would help me fix the scared part of me. It didn't. It just made me want you more. Then when you met Simon, I was for sure he would see what an awesome woman you were and was going to marry you for sure. Thank God, he was an idiot." He laughs.

I just sit and listen as he pours his heart out to me. This is the Wade I know and love and I can't wait to be his.

We got off the phone. It is really late. I am so tired. I don't even remember falling asleep.

The next day is the wedding.

I take Charlie out for his walk at the pet friendly hotel I found which had a groomer and boarding on site. I drop him off for a shampoo and cut which he really needs and sometime with other dogs.

I went and did some retail therapy at a few shops that were open and found a nice dress for the wedding even though I had already packed one. This one will look much better, I told myself.

I send my mom a picture of the dress. She responds with a heart emoji. I think about Wade as I see a couple holding hands while their toddler ran through the store. I can't wait for that to be Wade and me.

Megan's wedding is amazing — beautiful coral and white colors with gold accents, not to mention the beautiful orchids that lined the aisle when walked down. The entire time, I just envisioned me in the dress, me cutting the cake, and me sharing the first dance. I couldn't wait to get back home to wade.

The wedding was on the beach, outdoors which made it easy to social distance. Each person sat about two chair lengths away from each other, which made it difficult to see who didn't have a date.

I thought about Wade but that instantly brought thoughts about Charlie. I'm glad that Charlie was at the boarding place at the hotel. We really needed a break from each other. Especially ever since… I try to shake the thought of Charlie's tongue on me but I couldn't because he was there for me when no one else was.

What if he doesn't like Wade? What would I do? Get rid of him?

The music for the wedding started interrupting my thoughts as I stood to see Megan walk down the aisle. I was so happy for her.

As soon as the wedding was over, I was ready to get back to the room and talk to Wade. We had not spoken at all since staying up pretty much all night on the phone. I decided to keep Charlie in his boarding space so that Wade and I could have some alone time on the phone and I was not about to be interrupted.

"Hey, babe," he says when he answers my facetime. That makes me blush so hard plus the fact that Wade was sitting at is computer desk with his shirt off. I had to admit that beard he grew made him look even more delicious.

"Hey, Wade." Not knowing if we are back in the romantic name department, I just went with what I wanted. Wade.

I tell him about the wedding and he tells me how good I looked in the dress. I told him that I would look better without it on an began to take off my dress. One strap at a time.

I placed the phone down and began to do a strip tease for Wade. He was so quiet just staring at the screen.

"Are you going to join me?" I ask.

He smiled and stood only to show that he was already naked, showing his dick in his hand, giving it light strokes up and down. That made Mrs Kitty purr like never before.

"I haven't seen one of those in a while," I tell him, forcing him to laugh.

He says, "Good. you should be nice and tight for me when I see you tomorrow."

I was so glad that we were on the same page. I was so in need of some sex. We played and talked dirty until we both came.

After the clean-up, Wade asked, "Where is Charlie?"

I told him that he was spending the night at the boarding room that had at the hotel.

"I hope he recognizes me next time he sees me. I was thinking about shaving my beard so that he could be comfortable."

"No, Wade," I exclaimed, "keep the beard I love it, plus I haven't had a chance to play in it. Charlie will be fine. It's been so long since someone has even been in my house so I promise it will be fine. You and that beard just be at my place around 4 p.m. tomorrow. I will be checking out right at 11am so by 4 p.m. I should be home."

The night could not have gone slower. I felt like a kid waiting for Christmas morning.

I picked up Charlie around 9 a.m. He was so excited to see me. He jumped and ran circles around me. He even tried to sniff my crotch.

The guy who brought him said, "You two sure do have a special bond."

"Thanks," I said, knowing that statement was so true.

I stop by the breakfast bar. I pick up a bagel and an apple just something to hold me over until I got home. I was too nervous and excited to eat much. I grab my bags and Charlie and we hit the road to see my man.

I called my sister to give her the details on the wedding. She asked a thousand questions, giving her critique on weddings since she had already been married.

My sister's wedding was extravagant I must admit. She spent 135K on her wedding, sparing no expense since she and her ex-husband both were engineers.

You would have thought with that amount of money the wedding would have lasted at least one hundred and thirty-five months which is almost eleven years. They only made it to three.

"We were totally opposites, but not the ones that

attract," Tabitha told me when I asked what happened with her and Pete. He was out going and she was a homebody like my dad.

Now that Tabitha has been divorced, she has been trying to find her spontaneous side. It's working but it is a little too late because her husband was gone.

It was then I told myself that I would do any and everything to save my marriage — that's if I ever get into one.

We talked for about two hours which made the trip go even faster.

As we got closer, I started feeling little butterflies in my stomach.

I send Wade a text at a rest stop on the highway to give Charlie a bathroom break, letting him know I was two hours away. He said perfect and he couldn't wait to see me. I thought it was weird that he declined my facetime and opted for a phone call instead.

He rushed me off the phone and said, "See you soon, L.A."

That made me want to drive even faster. I was so ready to get home. I would have flown if I knew this was going to happen.

I called my mom and told her what Wade did. "Well, honey, it sounds like he's planning something big for you."

"I know, Mom, do you think he's going to propose?"

"Lauren, relax," she tells me. "There is no need for you to get your hopes up. You guys have just seen each other for the first time in months. Give him some time, honey, he's been through a lot this year. Rushing will only make things worse in the end, that's what I also told your sister and you see where that got her."

"You're right, Mom. I can always count on you for sound advice."

I began to tell her how Charlie acted when Wade came over the other day.

"Wow, he's really overprotective of you. Do you think he will try to hurt Wade?"

"I don't know, Mom," I say. "It was scary."

"Well, just give him time to adjust. It has just been you two, peas in a pod, during this entire pandemic. He was there for you when you needed him the most and that's all that matters," she says.

If she only knew how close we were.

We talk until I get into Atlanta city limits which meant I had only an hour drive left. I end the call with my mom, not knowing I would soon be calling her back.

I get home and grab my two bags and Charlie and we head to our home which I did miss. It was the only place I've been all 2020 so far.

I walk in and I see a nice size gift box on my dining room table. I drop my bags excitedly and went to the box. I open the box and it was a picture of my middle school and there was a note attached that said "where we met".

There was another box a bit smaller a photo of my parents' house. This note said "where we shared our first kiss". I was so excited because I knew where this was going.

But where was Wade?

I open the remaining boxes which were pictures of things and places we've experienced first. He even put a picture of his car where we first made love.

The last box was small about a ring size box. I open the box and it was a tiny piece of paper that said 'open the door'.

I drop the box and rushed back to the door and opened it, only to see Wade on his knees holding the most beautiful ring I had ever seen. I instantly began to cry. He had tears in his eyes as well.

He asks, "Lauren Anastasia Peterson, will you marry me?"

"Yes, Wade!" I say, "Yes, I'll marry you."

He picks me up and carries me inside, only to see Charlie standing and growling in front of him.

"Sit," I yell from the arms of my now Fiancé. He reluctantly goes to his pillow and sits but he is clearly not happy.

Wade walks back to my bedroom and lays me on the bed and closes the door. He says, "So, future Mrs Jameson, is it okay if we make this official and consummate our engagement?"

I say nothing, instead, I take off my sundress which shows I've had nothing under the entire time.

"I love your sexy ass," he says and takes off his shirt showing his broad shoulders and strong pecks. Then he lowered his pants and I can see his dick's outline through his boxers. I want to rip them off, but I am patient and let him do it.

He walks over to the bed naked as well. His dick looks so good, like it needs a kiss so I take him in my mouth as he stands. The taste of his dick is amazing. I forgot how much I missed it. I suck him slowly at first, getting him warmed up as he grabs my hair which is already in a ponytail.

I begin to gag on the girth of his dick but I don't care. This is my husband and I am going to please him every way imaginable.

He tells me to stop because he wanted to return the favor. He gets down on the bed and I lay back patiently, waiting for his tongue to meet my clit.

Before I close my eyes, I see a shadow at the foot of the door and it is Charlie. Do I say something? My mind begins to race. I try to relax.

I tell Wade to wait for a second and I tells Charlie to go to his chair. He begins to bark.

I get up, grab my robe and open the door. I grab Charlie by the collar and sat him outside on the balcony for the first time. I feel bad but mommy needs this alone time with no interruptions.

"What's gotten into him?" Wade jokes as I enter the room.

I ignore the question and ask him, "Where were we?"

He picks me up and lays me on my back and proceeds to talk to my pussy with his wet lips and strong tongue. They talk and talk until there is nothing else to say and I cum for my fiancé.

"That's what I wanted," he says.

He then flips me on to my stomach and I arch my ass that was clearly bigger from when he last saw it. He smacks my ass and grabs it, signaling his approval.

Wade slides inside of me and Mrs Kitty is in heaven. Each stroke makes me grab the sheets tighter and muffle my screams into the pillow.

I tried to gain some control and throw my ass back at him, but his stroke and weight is too strong, causing me to just take it as he strokes me into another orgasm.

I cum so hard that my pussy puts a grip on Wade that I guess he couldn't handle because seconds later he came all on my ass and back.

We lay and bask in our glory before we clean up.

While catching our breath, I ask Wade, "How did you get into my place?"

He said he went to my parents' house after he left me and asked for my hand in marriage. They were so happy for us and said they knew it would happen. He said he even saw my dad smile. "They gave me the spare key they had. Your mom talked all weekend about how we're going to plan this. She called right after you two got off the phone and told me that you were about an hour away. I came over, placed the box and waited across the street until I saw you park."

I laugh at how clueless I was. I can't believe my mom. She told me to relax and just wait, that marriage would come. All along she was in on this.

I look at the ring and say, "Wade, it's beautiful. I love it."

He says, "It's my mom's. She insisted that you have it."

"What?" I ask.

"Yeah," he says, "when I was there with my mom, she asked about you and wondered why we weren't together. I explained to her the role I played in our break up and she said 'Wade, don't let her get away.' Before my mother passed, she must have known it was going to happen. She took the ring off and said 'I want Lauren to have this. I know I was the special lady in your life but, just in case I don't make it, you make Lauren the next special lady in your life with this ring.' I cried in her arms like a baby. Because I wanted you but not at the cost of losing my mom. I had to accept that God is in control of all things and that I will see my mom again soon. I knew that I wanted you all my life and I'm glad that we finally have it."

Chapter 17

I sit in the gravel parking lot with tears in my eyes, wanting to drive away but I have to do this.

The PAWS Atlanta sign stares me in the face as I betray the one who has been with me when I was the loneliest. The cold gray skies aren't making this day any easier to deal as I sit and debate if I should drop Charlie off at this no kill animal shelter in the hopes that he will get adopted.

Things at home over the past few months haven't been great. Charlie has been out of control and it's my fault. I never should have let Charlie come into my bedroom. The first time he licked my thigh while I was masturbating, I knew I had gone too far. I regret the first time I let him taste Mrs Kitty. It felt so good at the time, not knowing the consequences that I would be facing at this moment in time.

Forced to choose between Charlie and Wade, my best friend or fiancé.

Charlie bit Wade last week and that was the last straw. Each time Wade would come over, I would have to put Charlie on the balcony.

Well, this one particular night, it was raining and cold and I didn't want him outside. Wade had come over after work and Charlie would not listen to me or him and, when Wade went to grab his collar. Charlie bit him on the hand.

Wade left and said, "LA, call me when you can get control of your dog."

This wasn't the only issue with Charlie. Each time Wade and I would make love, Charlie would bark and howl to the point where we just stopped having sex at my house.

Wade asked what was I going to do because, if were planning to start a family and raise kids, we could not do it with Charlie, even though he was trained.

"I know, I told him last week. I will find a shelter" and here I am. The fact is, that it's almost Thanksgiving, a time where you celebrate the ones you love not give them away to a shelter.

I look Charlie in the eyes, one blue and one green, and pat him on the head. I try not to let him lick me but this was probably going to be our last time seeing each other so I let him lick my hands and even my cheeks.

"I'm going to miss you Charlie, but I have to move on with my life and you acting aggressive towards Wade isn't making it any better," I tell him.

I open the car door and he leaps out on my side. I attach his leash and lead him inside.

"Yes, he's trained." I hand the woman at the counter his certificate from Obedience school.

"This will have him adopted in no time," the woman says. "Families love dogs that are already trained. Why are you giving him up?" she asks, looking confused considering how much I was just bragging about him to her.

"Well, I'm getting married and my fiancé is allergic to dogs," I lie. I can't tell her the truth. I let my dog taste my pussy and now he's acting crazy towards my fiancé. I would be on my Strange Addiction on TLC in no time.

She says, "That fiancé must be a hell of a catch because giving up a dog like this is something you just don't see."

"I know."

I sign the rest of the paperwork and give Charlie one last hug, trying to hold back the tears.

I walk back out into the cold.

I send Wade a text that says: dinner at my place tonight?

He quickly replies: What about Charlie?

I reply: he's taken care of see you at six.

I drive away, leaving the dark secret Charlie and I shared in the back of my mind, never having to worry about it again.